There are so many animals!
Some animals live free. They can
get the food and water they need.
We name them wild animals.

Wild animals include foxes, otters, owls, toads and blackbirds.

Farm animals such as sheep, turkeys, hens and cows give meat, eggs and milk.

Horses and donkeys have busy lives on farms, too.

Then there are animals we keep as pets. The long name for pets is domestic animals. (Domestic means in our homes.)

They bring a lot of joy and need a lot of looking after. Ferrets, rats, cats, fish and rabbits can all be happy pets.

Let me tell you about an animal
I am fond of. Hamsters! They are
merry, quick, lively, and so much
fun. My pretty hamster, Hammy,
has plenty of room to run and play.

She curls up in a nest of chippings to sleep in the day. At night she wakes up, still sleepy. She yawns so widely you can see her sharp teeth and her pink throat.

She drinks water from a bottle and
eats grain from a dish.

It took a while for Hammy to let me pick her up. At first, I spoke to her softly and let her smell my hand. Now that she trusts me, she will happily sit on my hand.

It makes me very, very happy to feel the soft pads of her dainty feet and her lovely, furry belly.

I have a dog, too. His name is
Monty. I didn't have him as a
puppy. He came to live with me
when he was five.

Until then, he ran on the dog track on his long, long legs. He still runs like he is swimming in the air, and he still runs in big loops if he can.

13

Monty is soft and more velvety than hairy. He is a dog who loves a hug. In fact, he is a real cuddle monster! You can tell he is asking for a hug by the way he lifts his nose and leans on your leg.

Many dogs enjoy water. Not Monty!
He drinks water.
But water as rain? No.
Water in a stream? No, thank you.
Water in the sea? No! No! No!

Funny old dog. He is a perfect
Monty, water or no water.
I love him just as he is.